MW00974647

* * *

ANNE ELIOT CROMPTON

The Snow Pony

*
* *
*

Henry Holt and Company   *   *New York*

First edition
Published by Henry Holt and Company, Inc.,
115 West 18th Street, New York, New York 10011.
Published simultaneously in Canada by Fitzhenry & Whiteside Ltd.,
195 Allstate Parkway, Markham, Ontario L3R 4T8.

Library of Congress Cataloging-in-Publication Data
Crompton, Anne Eliot.
    The snow pony / Anne Eliot Crompton.
    Summary: Moving to a small Massachusetts town and finding it
hard to make friends, thirteen-year-old Jannie takes a job with
Mr. Flower, "the mad hermit of Winterfield," helping him tame and
groom a pony.
    ISBN 0-8050-1573-6 (acid-free paper)
    [1. Loneliness—Fiction. 2. Friendship—Fiction. 3. Ponies—
Fiction. 4. Old age—Fiction.] I. Title.
PZ7.C879Sn   1991   90-23632
[Fic]—dc20

Henry Holt books are available at special discounts
for bulk purchases for sales promotions, premiums,
fund-raising, or educational use. Special editions
or book excerpts can also be created to specification.

Printed in the United States of America
on acid-free paper.∞

10 9 8 7 6 5 4 3 2 1

*This story is for Frances,
Adhi, Phoebe Jane, Alexander,
Jeremiah, and all readers.*

*

The Snow Pony

*
* *
*

* * * * * * * * * * * * * *1*

*I'*m ambling home from school down Hungry Hollow Road. Trees stretch gray fingers to the gray winter sky. Clouds hang low like my heart.

I've been in this new school here in Winterfield since Christmas, and I still haven't found one friend.

Back in Holyoke, where I come from, Maria was my friend. Maria was plump, like me. Her eyes and hair were black, where mine are brown. She laughed all the time, and didn't let me mope. Here in this lonesome, woodsy place I mope a lot.

There goes Marigold Stass waltzing along ahead of me. She hears me splashing slush behind her. Does she turn around, wave, wait up?

She does not. Nose high, she marches in the back door of her big old farmhouse on the left, and slams the door. Nobody in Winterfield uses their front door. That's just one of the weird things around here.

Hungry Hollow Road is a dirt road with ice furrows.

Woods close in on both sides. Bears and wolves stand in snow and grin at me. I look again, and they are branches and rocks. Back in Holyoke there were always lights and people. Winterfield is mostly spooky woods and snow.

The next house on the right is spookier than the woods. This is Mr. Flower's house.

Kids giggle or scowl when they say, "Mr. Flower." He's some kind of mad hermit. I've never seen him yet, and I don't think I want to.

His house is just a cabin. Low smoke drifts out of a pipe in the roof. The yard is fenced with leaning wood posts and chicken wire. An old, twisted apple tree with a tire swing stands in the middle of the yard.

I walk fast here, and watch the yard from the corner of my eye. I feel the cabin door may burst open any second, and Mr. Flower may peer out at me.

Holy trout! A bit of dirty gray snow is rolling about under the apple tree!

I walk more slowly, watching.

The dirty gray snow heaves and squirms and kicks four legs in the air.

Watching, I stop.

The snow scrambles up and shakes itself. It jumps up and down and turns into a small, shaggy horse. He tosses a wild mane out of wild eyes and swishes a matted tail. He snorts.

I jump.

The little horse looks fierce. But there's a fence between us. I'm safe. I move a bit closer, watching.

The horse paws the snow and shakes his head. He bucks, then trots around the apple tree. Without his coat of dirt he would be white as the snow pony the Stass kids made in their yard last week. Cleaned up and cared for, he might be pretty. But I don't like the way he lays his ears back and bares his long yellow teeth. I'm glad of the fence between us.

A voice in my ear says, "You're the new girl."

I whirl. A stooped old man stands just inside the fence. He wears patched jeans and a huge patched sweater. Smiling through his white beard, he says, "You're Janet Stone. Your mother teaches at the high school. Correct?"

I back off. I prickle and blush as always when I meet someone new. But I manage to say, "That's right."

"You like my Pearl." He nods toward the fierce little horse.

"I—he's . . . cute." I don't add that he's the first living, breathing horse I've ever seen close up.

"I got him at the auction for my grandson, Arthur. Arthur's ten. Are you ten, Janet Stone?"

"I'm thirteen." Can't he see that? I'm big enough, too!

"I'm Russ Flower," says the old man. "You want to meet my Pearl?"

"Well, no, I—"

Mr. Flower marches over to Pearl and grabs a rope halter almost buried in fur. Pearl snaps his teeth and digs his hoofs into snow. Pearl doesn't want to meet me. Mr. Flower drags him up to the fence anyhow. Pearl glares at me.

Mr. Flower says, "Pearl's shy. He's had some rough handling somewhere, and maybe no handling at all for a while. But we'll straighten him out good for Arthur."

A horse should be beautiful. Pearl is ugly. His coat stands out stiff and filthy, his back caves in, he's got leathery flaps on his stubby legs and a scowl on his face.

Mr. Flower says, "Let him smell your hand, Janet. Then you can pat him."

"No thanks, I—"

"Come on! Somebody has to make the first move, and it won't be Pearl."

I don't see why either of us has to make the first move.

Quick as a snake, Mr. Flower grabs my hand and shoves it under Pearl's nose. Pearl and I both pull back so hard we jerk loose. Pearl snorts, wheels, and tears off, spattering snow.

Mr. Flower asks, "What do you think? You want the job?"

"Job?"

"Well, see, Pearl needs a lot of work to get ready for Arthur. He needs gentling, grooming, feeding. I can do all that. Then he needs riding, training, exercise, and I can't do that. Someone your size has to do that. I'll pay two . . . two fifty . . . three dollars an hour. Every day after school. What do you say?"

I'm too surprised to answer.

"Three fifty an hour. Can't go any higher."

There's a snowstorm of confusion in my head! "Fact is," I mumble, "I don't know all that much about horses."

Mr. Flower grins through his beard. "Don't you worry, Janet Stone! I'll show you about horses!"

I used to want to call Jackie "Mom." She wouldn't let me. "I don't call you 'Daughter,' " she would say. "Why should you call me 'Mom'? My name's Jackie."

Jackie's my height, but heavier. She wears jeans and sweaters everywhere, even at the high school where she teaches shop. This used to embarrass me in Holyoke, where other mothers went to work in high heels. But here in Winterfield Jackie fits right in. Her brown-gray hair hangs in a thick braid to her hips. Her square hands are always busy. I think she bought this rattle-trap farmhouse to keep our hands busy fixing it up. It sure is a comedown from the neat apartment we had in Holyoke. It was small, but the plumbing worked.

We moved here from Holyoke so Jackie could teach at the regional high school. We moved to Holyoke so Jackie could go to school so she could learn how to teach shop. Before that we lived with my dad in Hartford. A tractor-trailer hit my dad, and he's dead. I don't remember him.

Jackie has a snapshot of him on her bureau. He's in army uniform, and he's leaning against a car on a bright street, with his arm around Jackie. He looks thin, but she's half in front of him, so I can't be sure.

To know a person's looks you have to see him front, back, and side, in different clothes, doing different things. I can only see my dad leaning against a car on a bright street with his arm around Jackie.

I tend to look sharp at dads. Once I saw Maria's dad. He was small and quiet and dark. Maria said whenever he got mad he turned into a whole different person.

I've seen Marigold's dad. He's short and heavy, with big hands. I've heard him roar, "Marigold!" or "Sophie!" or "Frankie!" I've heard him laugh, too.

I don't remember my dad's face or hands or voice. All I know is, he liked to draw pictures, like me. But the pictures are all lost.

Now Jackie and I are scraping pink paint off a high cupboard. I kneel on the kitchen counter. Jackie stands on a chair.

"So, Jannie," she says loudly, over the scrape-scrape, "what do you think? Do you want the job?"

"I think so." It would be better than coming home to an empty house every day. Jackie doesn't get home till five.

"I went to see your Mr. Flower," Jackie says. "I saw your Pearl, too. They're about equally odd."

"Did you see Pearl's teeth, the better to bite me with?"

"Aha! Mr. Flower will teach you how to handle Pearl. That's what I like about this job for you—you'll learn a lot."

So she won't stop me working for Mr. Flower! He didn't scare her off. I say, "I like the three fifty an hour myself."

"Money never hurts. But there's one thing, Jannie." Jackie tosses her swinging braid back over her shoulder. "You're to stay outdoors."

"Well, sure. I'll be working outdoors."

"I don't want you inside that cabin, or the shed. Ever."

"What shed?"

"It looks like part of the cabin. Pearl lives in it."

"OK, I won't go inside. But why not?"

"Because we don't know Mr. Flower."

"Holy trout, Jackie, we don't know anybody!"

"He seems like a harmless old man minding his own business. But we'd better be careful. After all, he might be a werewolf."

"A what?"

"Maybe when the moon is full he turns into a wolf."

"Oh, Jackie!"

"You'll always be safe outdoors. You can run faster than Mr. Flower."

"I can jump on Pearl and gallop away."

"After Mr. Flower shows you how. Careful with that scraper, Jannie, you're gouging the wood."

* * * * * * * * * * * * * *3*

I keep a pad, pencil, and markers by my bed. Sometimes, before I sleep, I draw a picture. Tonight, I draw my new job. Pearl.

I start with his head, his beady eyes and snappy teeth. This almost scares me. I crumple that sheet and start over. I draw Pearl jumping around in snow. The way he moves, I know he can be pretty. Under that dirty winter coat of his, he's got style.

This isn't Mr. Flower's Pearl after all. It's a snow-white Lippizaner stallion, dancing on his hind feet. His mane and tail float like dandelion fluff. When I pencil in shadows, his sleek coat shines. This is OK!

Now on his back . . . is me. I'm thin. I sit up straight and hold the reins gracefully, in one hand. My pants—I mean jodhpurs—are brown, like my boots.

My coat is . . . blue. All around us I color black clouds, which make the stallion shine whiter.

There. That's OK. Another touch would spoil it.

I leave the pad open by my bed. First thing I'll see in the morning will be me on a snow-white horse. My new job.

*J*hate recess.

Back in Holyoke it wasn't this bad because my friend Maria was with me. Maria is round and brown. She has black eyes that spark, and a cloud of black hair that can crackle. She has a warmth in her that helps you to feel good even when you don't.

Maria and I would sit on the school steps at recess and watch the boys rush around like savages and the girls gossip in knots. And after a while this warmth of Maria's would steal over me, and I would turn to her and talk.

Maria got left out of the gossip knots because she talked funny, and wore real silver earrings that swung, and her brothers were sort of wild, always getting in fights.

I got left out because Jackie wouldn't buy all the stuff you needed to be in one of those knots. You needed a big floppy sweater and printed leggings.

You needed a magnetic notebook, orange sneakers, a beaded headband, something new every week. My allowance wouldn't stretch for all that. And Jackie tossed back her braid and snorted, "Hah! Forget it!"

She didn't have to explain to me. I knew how much money she made, and how much we spent for rent and hamburger and gas and all that. We just couldn't manage printed leggings.

Now here I am in Winterfield, all by myself without Maria. I'm cold inside and out, and recess is the worst part of my day.

All the eighth-grade girls are in the Marigold Stass group. They cluster around Marigold as if she's the Queen and they are all her Court. Fat Tunie, Cute Irene, and Tough Jessie stand closest to Marigold. The rest form a circle with me outside it.

Marigold is telling a Cliff story. "Cliff turned his ankle last night so he couldn't change the tire. I had to change it for him."

Cliff is Marigold's boyfriend. He gave her the red, gleaming Friendship Ring she always wears. He goes to high school and drives his dad's Chevy. Everyone knows all that, but no one has met Cliff. And no one else has a boyfriend.

"We were coming home from the movie," Marigold says, "and the tire blew on Indian Hill."

Cute Irene purrs, "What were you doing on Indian Hill anyhow?"

Tough Jessie growls, "Not on your way, exactly."

Marigold tosses her golden curls. "Never you mind. Anyhow, there we were, midnight—"

"Come on, Marigold!" Fat Tunie pops her bubble gum.

"OK, maybe ten thirty. Late. And the tire blows. And Cliff's got this swelled ankle, he can't hardly drive with it. So he gets to hold the flashlight and I change the tire."

Tunie asks through gum, "He told you how, blow-by-blow description?"

"My dad taught me to change a tire before I could push one. My little brother Frankie can change a tire!"

The Court sighs an admiring sigh. I don't know how to change a tire myself, though Jackie does.

Cute Irene asks, "Did you wear the blue dress you made?"

"Sure I did! Cliff noticed it matched my eyes." I'm not much for sewing, either.

Pale winter sunshine flashes on Marigold's curls, on her red Ring, and on the admiring faces of her Court. I shift my freezing feet and sigh.

Later I'll walk home alone down Hungry Hollow

Road. Marigold will march ahead, nose to sky, pretending I'm nowhere near. All alone I'll come to our new, old house that needs so much work. The house will be loud with silence, full of emptiness.

But then! Then I'll tear into my jeans and trot back to work for Mr. Flower!

When kids say, "Mr. Flower," they wrinkle their noses as though his name was "Mr. Skunk." I don't see anything that bad about him.

He's old and twisted up. Jackie says that's from years of very hard work.

He likes to talk. No one here would believe how much Mr. Flower talks to me! Jackie says that's because he's lonesome.

He's crazy about his grandson, Arthur. I don't believe half of what he says about Arthur. I don't believe Arthur is the smartest boy in his whole school, or that he won first prize in Massachusetts for figure skating, or that he saved a baby from a fire.

But Jackie says Mr. Flower believes all that. "He's just crazy about his grandson. He thinks about him all the time." I wonder if my Grandpa Stone, who lived out in San Francisco, was ever that crazy about me.

Mr. Flower says that between us we can make Pearl beautiful and gentle for Arthur, so Arthur will rejoice to see him. We can turn suspicious, bad-tempered Pearl into a dream pony.

Thinking about that I feel almost warm. Queen Marigold Stass and her Court almost fade away in the winter sunshine.

Wait for me, Pearl! I'm coming to work with you!

* * * * * * * * * * * * * *5

*M*r. Flower says, "Hold him good, Janet. Like this, under his chin."

"But he's tied, Mr. Flower."

Pearl is crosstied. Two ropes lead from his halter to two far-apart iron staples in the outside shed wall. He stands rigid, but his eyes have a wicked glow.

" 'Course he's tied! But you want to hold his head right up, else I might get kicked."

I hold Pearl under his chin. He shivers, and I can't help but sympathize. He has no idea what these two humans are going to do.

Snow spits down from the low gray sky. Posy, the old white tomcat, sits curled on the inside of the open shed window, watching us. His ears and tail twitch. Posy, too, wonders what we're doing.

"It's OK," I murmur in Pearl's ear, "we're just going to take off your warts." Mr. Flower calls those leathery flaps on Pearl's front legs "warts."

Mr. Flower crouches in snow. In mittened hands he grips a pair of huge scissors. "These are trimmers," he says. "Mostly I use them on raspberries, but they'll do this job."

Pearl's right eye glares down at those trimmers. His ears turn back. I wouldn't want those used on me either!

Mr. Flower says, "My grandson, Arthur, read a book in school about horses. Wrote a paper on it." With one slow, steady crunch he slices off the first wart. "Arthur got an A."

In my book, Mr. Flower gets an A! Pearl doesn't seem to notice the cut.

"See, doesn't hurt. Like cutting toenails. Now we just trim up a bit. . . ."

He fishes a knife out of his jeans and flicks ragged wart edges off Pearl's leg.

"They sent Arthur's horse paper for me to see. That's why I thought to buy Pearl for Arthur."

"Who sent you the paper, Mr. Flower?"

"Stephen, of course. My son."

"I didn't know you had a son."

"Glory, how would I have a grandson without I had a son?"

"Well, you might have a daughter."

"Ha ha, that's true!" Scrape, scrape. "No, I've just got my son, Stephen. And Stephen's got Arthur."

"Is Stephen married, Mr. Flower?"

"Married. Oh my yes, Stephen is married."

Mr. Flower flicks the knife shut and drops it in his pocket. He runs his mittened hand over the black mark where the wart was, and up and down Pearl's leg. Pearl snorts and stamps.

"Now to get up." Mr. Flower struggles. I reach a hand to him. He slaps it away. My hand doesn't hurt, but my feelings do. I stand and watch him fight his way up.

He rests a hand on Pearl's rump and moves behind him. There he pauses and says, "Janet, when you go behind Pearl, touch him. Let him know you're there. If you startle him, he'll kick."

In the shed window, Posy yawns. A bearded, horned head pushes out beside him. Rosy, the old white goat, watches us with narrow yellow eyes.

Mr. Flower crouches beside me, trimmers ready. Pearl jerks his head restlessly. "Hold his foot up, Janet. Like that. Now he can't move, see."

Pearl can't move because he's off-balance, and so am I. "We'll be through in a minute now." I hope so!

Slow, steady *crunch*. Out comes the knife. Scrape, scrape.

Mr. Flower says, "When the apple tree blooms, Arthur will come."

Off-balance and bowed over, I peer up at the apple

tree. Falling snow mounds up on its bare, twisted buds. I suppose they will bloom in the spring, but that's hard to imagine right now.

Mr. Flower says, "Pearl will be different by then. Arthur will rejoice to see him! He'll have his summer coat, short and shiny. And he'll be tame." That's even harder to imagine.

Mr. Flower clambers up, claps a hand to his back. "Oof!"

I let go of Pearl. He shakes his head and backs as far as the crossties will stretch. He and Mr. Flower look at each other. Pearl looks angry, Mr. Flower looks thoughtful. Snow falls like cotton balls on Pearl's mane and Mr. Flower's beard.

"Well," Mr. Flower says, "that's a job done. We've commenced." And he unclips Pearl's crossties.

Pearl bares his teeth at us. Then he whirls and trots away to the fence. From there he watches us suspiciously.

"We've got a way to go, Janet, before the apple tree blooms!"

I'll say!

* * * * * * * * * * * * * *6*

I wake early in the cold dark. A dream sticks to me.

After a quick trip down to the bathroom I huddle back under my quilt and draw the dream.

A dog, a German shepherd, stands on two legs. Ears perk, tongue lolls, eyes gleam. (Erase, draw, erase.) She leans far forward, almost off-balance, looking down at something. Oh, she's got teeth. Sharp teeth. She wears a coat, pants, boots.

Next to him, a cat stands on two legs. A kittenish cat. Pink bow behind the ears, pink dress, high heels. Higher heels. Aha. She smiles, and she's got teeth. And whiskers. She leans way over like the dog, looking down. Studying something.

Facing them, a bunny on two legs. She leans forward and studies like the others. One ear flops up, the other down. Gum balloons out of her grin. Her huge tent of a coat touches her boot tops.

And here in the middle, what they all study and gawk at . . . a hand, palm down, fingers spread, shows off the Ring.

It covers the whole middle finger and reaches up half the hand. Red, red, red. Yellow rays and blue rays shoot off from it to touch the three quivering, eager noses.

This is one crazy drawing. The gleam in Dog's eye is good, and so is Cat's smile. I like Bunny's lifelike ears, and I'm very proud of the hand. I guess I'll save it for those good bits. But the whole picture—Dog, Cat, Bunny, and Ring—is nuts. What can you expect if you draw a dream?

* * * * * * * * * * * * * * * 7

*M*r. Flower says, "Commence at the top. Work the currycomb back and down."

He starts on Pearl's neck. "Not his face, see. Nor his lower legs. Currycomb's too harsh." Mr. Flower combs in circles. Dust and dirt fly, drift, and fall out of Pearl's ragged coat.

Crosstied to the shed wall, Pearl paws the snow. His left eye gleams at me, bright with wicked thoughts. He would love to bite!

In the shed window, Posy Cat grooms himself.

Rosy Goat bounds about the yard. I never saw Rosy when I used to walk by, because she stayed in the shed. She hates wet and mess. But now in springlike sunshine she leaps up and down on her rock pile. I never noticed the rock pile either. Thought it was just drifted snow. But Mr. Flower built it for Rosy to hop on, sharpen her hoofs, play Queen of the Castle.

He also hung the tire in the apple tree for Rosy.

Now she attacks it. She dances around on her hind legs and butts it.

Mr. Flower says, "You do his shoulder," and hands me the currycomb.

I stand back out of reach of Pearl's eager teeth and take a deep breath. What with all this dirt flying, I won't want to breathe again for a while. I begin to comb.

Pearl sighs and shifts his weight. Suddenly, he relaxes. "Look at that!" says Mr. Flower. "He likes what you do for him. Pretty soon he'll like you, too."

That will take a while. But I feel myself almost liking Pearl. I like helping him look and feel better. His new trustful relaxation warms my heart.

The snow under us is turning brown.

Mr. Flower says, "Your mom stops in to say hi now and then."

"She does!"

"Doesn't seem my idea of a schoolteacher."

"Well, she teaches shop."

"I never went in much for school, or teachers. See, it was like this. . . ."

Pearl's ears perk back and forth. He thinks Mr. Flower is talking to him.

"I was bright enough. I could read and write and reckon. But to graduate, you had to recite a poem, Decoration Day.

"They hung daisy chains all over the room, and put flowers around on desks, and asked the folks in. The school was just the one room then."

"One room?"

"Correct. You know the town office building next to the post office?"

I nod. It's a one-room affair. Jackie and I went there to look up papers when we bought our house.

"That was the school. No plumbing, neither."

"Holy trout, what did you have?"

"Two outhouses, behind lilac bushes. So anyhow, we had to recite, in front of everybody. A poem, or the Gettysburg Address, or 'When in the course of human events.' So. There you have it. I'll take over."

Mr. Flower begins to comb on Pearl's right side.

I think I've missed something. "What do you mean, Mr. Flower?"

"Well. How would you like to recite a poem to a room full of everybody's folks?"

I prickle and blush at the thought! "What did you recite?"

"Didn't. I knew the poem. I know it to this day. It commenced,

" *'I wandered lonely as a cloud*
That floats on high o'er vales and hills,

When all at once I saw a crowd,
A host of golden daffodils.'

"You know the one."

"Sounds pretty." But I don't know it.

"It's Wordsworth. English poet." Mr. Flower stops combing. He looks at me over Pearl's shoulder, through a dust cloud.

"Could you stand under an American flag and a daisy chain all by yourself and recite that to the minister's wife, and your great-aunt Mildred who thinks you're lacking"—he touches his forehead—"and Mrs. Winterfield in a silk dress, and all your neighbors, and your mom's clenching her fists in her lap, she's so scared you'll forget? Could you recite, Janet Stone?"

I blush and prickle. "I don't know. What did you do?"

"Walked out."

"Walking out would scare me more than reciting!"

"I was scared. But I couldn't recite."

"But then you didn't graduate!"

"Correct. Never did. I walked out of that school and went fishing. Sometimes I think I've been fishing ever since."

* * * * * * * * * * * * *8*

$\mathcal{F}$riday at recess, Marigold says, "Cliff says SHE works for Mr. Flower!"

The Court groans. "Mr. Flower?" "Mr. Hermit?" "Mr. Weirdo?" And they all draw away from me as if I smell.

Marigold pokes her snub nose at the sky and says, "Cliff says SHE helps him with that fleabag sway-backed old pony he got at the auction." The Court murmurs and shakes its head.

I don't know how Marigold's Cliff knows anything about me, and right now I don't care. I won't have old Pearl insulted like this! I say right out, "He's not so bad. He just needs some cleaning up and feed-ing."

Marigold stares at me. "Who?" she asks. "Who needs cleaning and feeding—Mr. Flower or his pony?" The Court explodes laughing.

Tough Jessie barks, "Why didn't he hire you, Marigold? At least you know something about horses!"

Marigold twirls her Friendship Ring on her finger. It sparkles in winter sunlight. "Probably knew I had better things doing," she says.

Tunie pops gum. She jerks her head at me. "*She* know anything about horses?"

Marigold shrugs.

I button my mouth and stare at Tunie. There's no point trying to talk to these Winterfield kids.

"Anyway," Cute Irene purrs, "where did you and Cliff go this time?"

Marigold starts a new story about Cliff at a bowling alley. I don't even pretend to listen. I wander off kicking slush, missing Maria.

I pretend she's slushing alongside me in her brother's old boots. If I pretend hard enough I can almost feel her friendly warmth.

"Girl!" she says. "That Marigold kid is wild! I'd like to, you know, straighten her hair for her."

"Oh, Maria, I wish you could! I wish I could see you, or write you a letter."

"So write."

"I sent you a card last Christmas. It came back. You never got it."

"Oh, right! We moved."

I stop kicking slush. I stand still by the fence and look down at the slush and think: Maria will never write and tell me where she is. Maria doesn't write letters, or draw pictures, or fuss anyhow with paper. I'm the one who does that.

I think: I've really lost Maria for good.

∗ ∗ ∗ ∗ ∗ ∗ ∗ ∗ ∗ ∗ ∗ *9*

"*J*anet Stone! Don't you never, ever wrap that lead around your wrist!"

I'm trying to lead Pearl around the yard through lazy snow showers. He keeps stopping to snatch at tufts of dead grass, or to nuzzle his side, or toss his head. I'm supposed to persuade him along, without ever letting on that he's stronger than I am.

Keeping to his left, I hold the lead close up to his chin with my right hand. I should hold the slack in my left hand, but it's easier to wrap it around my wrist.

Mr. Flower limps over to us on the run. He catches us as we turn at the fenced-in raspberry patch, and snatches the slack off my wrist. "That's how I lost my fingers," he says.

"What!"

"I've told you before, this here Pearl is a strong little fellow. If he took off sudden he could drag you to kingdom come before you got that lead off your wrist."

"Your fingers?"

Mr. Flower yanks off his left mitten and shows me his hand. It's a hard, skinny old hand, gnarled like the apple tree. The second and third fingers are stumps. Mr. Flower pulls his patched mitten back on.

"Lead him around the fence. Away from you. Always push, never pull. You want your toes squashed?" Pearl's small hoofs are heavy.

I nudge Pearl's chin, say, "Tl tl," and we're off. Mr. Flower trudges along with us, around the raspberries and behind the shed. He says, "That was neatly done."

"Seems like it's getting easier."

"You and Pearl are getting accustomed."

Well, that's true. We're not exactly friends yet, but we're not enemies either. Pearl no longer glares at me suspiciously. I don't worry so much about him biting. Now I wonder if Mr. Flower will bite if I ask him what I'm dying to ask.

"Mr. Flower," I ask softly, cautiously, "what happened with your fingers?"

"Accident."

I didn't think he did it on purpose! But Mr. Flower and I are getting accustomed. Sometimes, like Pearl, he needs to be persuaded along.

"An accident with a horse?"

"Ox."

"Ox!"

"Back then, see, the farmers mostly worked horses or oxen. No tractors. Roly LeDuc had a beautiful matched Jersey ox team, Bill and Bob. How that pair stepped out together! Didn't need gas like a tractor, or oil neither. Bill and Bob won blue ribbons every Cummington Fair."

"But Mr. Flower, your hand!"

"Let a man tell a story, Janet. Well, I worked for LeDuc. You know the LeDuc farm?"

I shake my head.

"Corner of Indian Hill and Southampton Road. Now it's all houses. Back then it was pasture, mowings, sugar brush.

"I worked there twenty years. Drove the vegetables down to Northampton, sold 'em door to door. Stop him here."

Mr. Flower stops. I pull back on Pearl's lead and holy trout, he stops, dead in his tracks! Mr. Flower pats his neck.

"Mr. Flower, you were saying . . ."

"I cut firewood all winter. And come sugar time, I sugared. Sugared all day, all night, while the sap flowed. Drove Bill and Bob from tree to tree up and down that hill, lifting sap pails."

It doesn't matter that I don't know what he's talking about. On with the story!

"Well, you get tired like that. You get so you don't

know what you're up to. That's why I wrapped the reins around my fingers.

"It was dawn, snow dusting down like now. I did the last tree and we started downhill to the sugarhouse. I was hungry. I thought about the sandwich in my pocket. I wrapped the reins around those two fingers and reached for the sandwich, and Bill stumbled.

"He hit a hole or rock, something under the snow. He stumbled and went down, and Bob lunged ahead. And the reins ripped my fingers out. That's what happened."

My fingers hurt.

"OK, Janet. Take him over to the apple tree."

I lead Pearl toward the tree. Mr. Flower keeps pace with us.

"You know, it's near sugar time now. I'll commence when the crows call, maybe next week. You can help."

"Me? I don't know how." In fact, I don't know what we're talking about.

"To hear you talk, you don't know much! Come on, Janet. You don't want me to hire that smart Marigold Stass next door!"

Holy trout, no! "I'll do it, Mr. Flower."

* * * * * * * * * * * *10*

*S*aturday morning, sunshine streams in our kitchen windows. I'm drawing at the table, pretending I don't hear Jackie bustling about in the broom closet.

I draw a boy sitting on a bank. His back is turned. He holds a fishing pole, a . . . sapling, with little branches. A line leads from its tip down to the water, which we don't see. (Water is hard to draw.)

The boy's head is bent. Beside him I draw a straw hat. Long ago, boys wore hats like this. I've seen them in books.

Jackie rattles in, a pail in each hand. She glances at my picture. Without comment, she fills the pails at the sink.

A leafy apple tree leans over the boy. Beside him I draw a . . . cat. He sits with his back to me, ears alert, tail twitching. He's a white cat, but I smudge him with penciled shadows. I smudge the boy, too, and the tree trunk. This is OK.

Jackie pulls two chairs up to the wall and sets the full pails between them. She goes back to the broom closet.

Quickly, tongue in my teeth, I draw a white goat. She rears up to nibble the tree. I give her horns, a flowing beard, and a full-to-bursting milk bag, I mean udder. I smudge her with shadows. This is OK.

Jackie looks over my shoulder again. "Good," she says. "Old-fashioned."

"That's because of the straw hat."

"Right. Takes us back fifty years! Here's your sponge, Jannie."

Jackie takes the long-handled mop. We climb on our chairs and attack the dirty wall. It does not clean easily.

Jackie asks, "Why the straw hat? Why fifty years ago?"

"I guess because . . . it's Mr. Flower."

"Aha! The hermit's been telling you his childhood?"

"Yes, he has. Did you know, Jackie, he never finished school?"

I tell her about "I wandered lonely as a cloud" and young Russ Flower fishing.

"Aha," she says, more softly. She lays her swinging braid back over her shoulder. "Hm. Never graduated.

Never could get a good job. Maybe that's why he's got a hot-poker temper."

"Hot-poker temper? Mr. Flower?" I'm surprised.

"Kids talk about him in shop. They call him the Mad Hermit of Winterfield. But Jannie, you know how kids talk! Probably not a word of truth in it."

Mop and sponge swish together. Water and detergent drip. Jackie says, "Catch your drips, Jannie, or we'll be looking at streaks till fall cleaning." She means, "Or we'll have to do this job over again." Jackie would never, ever leave streaks on the wall till fall cleaning!

Thoughtfully she adds, "You just stay outdoors at Mr. Flower's so you can take off fast."

"If he turns into a werewolf?"

"Or the Mad Hermit of Winterfield."

* * * * * * * * * * * * *11*

*M*r. Flower says, "Pearl's ready to ride."

I stop just inside the gate. "I don't know if I'm ready to ride!"

"Look at him! Tame as Posy!"

Pearl ambles up to let me pat his neck and blow in his nose. Purring Posy twines about our feet. Rosy comes bounding and pushes her head into Mr. Flower's hands. He rubs her ears.

Pearl doesn't bite now. He looks almost pretty. His thinning coat has a silver sheen. His mane and tail lift softly on the almost-spring breeze. He mumbles to me as though he likes me.

But I like my boots planted firmly in snow, not dangling in air! I say, "I'm not sure I'm ready to ride yet, Mr. Flower."

"Three fifty an hour, Janet." That's the deal. Mr. Flower pays, I ride.

A very old bridle swings from the apple tree. Mr. Flower hands it to me. "I cut this down from one my dad used. See, it's all greased and soft. Take off your gloves and warm the bit in your hands. Pearl don't want cold steel in his mouth."

I clasp the cold bit in my hands. "How long since he's been ridden?" Has he forgotten what he's supposed to do?

"We don't know that he ever has been." Holy trout! "Most likely so, but not for a long time. Maybe only babies rode him. Lots of small ponies never get the training we're going to give Pearl."

Oh me oh my. What am I about to do for three fifty an hour?

"Where's the saddle?"

"What for you want a saddle? You don't have far to fall." Happy thought! Mr. Flower's eyes cloud over dreamily. "I bet Stephen will buy a saddle for Arthur. Western, I bet, with a saddle blanket embroidered all pretty."

Maybe I can put off riding a moment more! "Mr. Flower," I ask, "where does Arthur live?"

"Castlebridge, over Boston way. OK town. Grass and trees. Fields around. Arthur will rejoice to ride in those fields!" Mr. Flower's eyes sharpen up. "Hey, what are we doing talking? We've got work cut out."

He grasps Pearl's chin and shoves a mittened thumb

in his mouth. The yellow teeth open like gates, and in goes the bit. Pearl champs it while Mr. Flower adjusts buckles here and there. "Show you this trick later on the fence. No use practicing on old Pearl. He's been bridled before, no problem with that. OK, Janet, up you go."

Mr. Flower's hands close on my waist. I'm a big girl, but he swings me up like a sack of feed.

And here I sit, on Pearl.

"Take your reins."

"Can't."

"Let go his mane. Hold the reins. Palms down. Good grip, that's right. I didn't realize I'd be training the two of you!"

"You said you would. You said, 'I'll show you about horses, Janet Stone.' "

"Right, so I did. Hold on with your knees. You're almost too tall for him. Now I'm going to lead him."

Oof. Uff. Pearl's shoulders—withers—move. His rump—croup—moves differently. I sway between the two. Good thing the ground is not too far down! If I could loosen my knees I could stretch a toe and touch snow.

"We're going to turn here, Janet."

Made it.

We walk the whole yard, past the fenced raspberry patch, the fenced garden patch, the shed, the cabin, all around the fence. We turn and go the other way. Rosy trots around us, interested ears twitching. Posy watches from the shed roof, tail tip twitching. I'm getting accustomed, swaying in a whole new motion, like a dance. This is OK.

Mr. Flower lets go of Pearl.

Pearl hesitates.

Lightly, Mr. Flower slaps his rump, I mean his croup, and says, "Tl tl." Pearl and I walk on. This is OK.

We pass the apple tree, heading for the woods. How to turn Pearl? Pull the rein. Gently, cautiously, I pull the left rein and let up on the right one.

Holy trout! Pearl turns! We walk around the tree and back toward Hungry Hollow Road. I want to whoop my surprised delight, but that would startle Pearl.

We plod toward the road. Mr. Flower stands stooped by the fence, grinning. Out on the road stand Marigold Stass and her little brother Frankie, and their huge black dog.

* * * * * * * * * * * * *12*

*M*arigold and Frankie are looking for empty bottles to take to the store. Marigold has on her new brown shoulder bag and a small camera hung around her neck. Frankie's got a plastic bag full of empties. They stare at Pearl and me as if they've never seen a horse and rider before.

My heart swells up like a balloon. Look, I want to shout, Look at me, Janet Stone! Me, Jannie! Look what I'm doing!

I feel as if Pearl is a prancing Lippizaner fifteen hands high, and I'm dressed in jodhpurs and shiny boots. How great that Marigold came by just now, when for once I'm doing fine!

I would like to send her a friendly, careless wave, but I'm gripping the reins too hard. Pearl and I plod quietly forward.

Little Frankie opens his mouth and points to us. He says something.

Marigold opens her mouth. She's going to call hello!

Marigold throws back her head. She's going to shout her amazed admiration for Janet Stone! I smile at her.

Marigold bursts into shrieks of whinnying laughter.

Marigold is not amazed, admiring, or impressed. Pearl and I are not impressive. We are a shaggy little pony and a big girl whose feet almost touch the snow.

Marigold screeches laughter. Laughter folds her up. She slaps her knees, arches her back. Laughter bursts out of Frankie, too. The two of them sound like hiccuping sirens. The dog sits down and howls.

Pearl jerks tight. His muscles bunch. He flings himself up and sideways. He spins around, tossing his mane in my face. He jumps up and down on his hind feet. This is not OK. I hold on with knees and feet and my fists in his mane. Forget the reins.

Stasses, be quiet! Don't you see you're spooking Pearl?

Shriek, screech!

Pearl thuds down into a dead run. I shut my eyes. We bound, we gallop, we jump something. Is this old Pearl churning snow, leaning into a bend, gallumphing, snorting? I hold on. *I will not fly off in front of Marigold Stass!*

Hey. He's slowing down.

I hear "Whoooa" in Mr. Flower's gentlest tone.

We skid to a stumbling stop.

Firm hands hold Pearl. I open my eyes. Mr. Flower grips the halter. Pearl trembles and pants. I want to slide down right now and plant my boots in safe snow. But I don't.

"That's the ticket," Mr. Flower croons, patting Pearl's neck. "You just sit tight. What did you do with the reins?"

I point. The reins loop limply down Pearl's heaving sides.

"Never let your reins go, Janet. Pearl could trip and break his neck."

The black dog's howls die off into hiccups. I steal a furious glance at Marigold. She lifts her camera and takes my picture, I think. She and Frankie stagger away laughing, the dog at their heels.

Frankie jumps sideways and swings his bottle bag. Like Pearl he whirls and hops and takes off at a gallop. The dog bounds and barks. The bottles in the bag rattle like laughter.

* * * * * * * * * * * * *13*

"*J*ackie," I say, "I don't want to go back to school!"

Jackie nods. "Because Queen Marigold will tell her Court about you and Pearl."

We're stripping wallpaper in my room. I kind of like the old wallpaper, with its big pink roses and blue bows, but it's stained brown and peeling, and Jackie says the big print makes my small room seem smaller.

I sponge the wallpaper with vinegar water and Jackie scrapes it off. Sometimes the paper lifts off in sheets. Sometimes she has to fight it.

Pulling off a sheet she says, "But what's to tell, Jannie? You rode Pearl for the first time. You didn't fall off, even when Marigold and Frankie spooked Pearl. What can Marigold tell the Court?"

"She'll make it funny," I say gloomily. "She'll have them rolling in the snow. Remember, I'm really too big for Pearl. I bet if I hadn't been on him myself, I might think it was funny!"

Jackie snorts and tosses her swinging braid back. "Maybe you could laugh a bit yourself."

"Laugh?"

"Sure. Join in. That might snip Queen Marigold's sting."

Soaking a big pink rose with vinegar, I think about that. It might work. But the thought of all those hard faces . . . "They'll be laughing *at* me, Jackie. Not *with* me."

"Turn it around."

"If Tough Jessie and Cute Irene and Fat Tunie will let me."

"I hope you don't say those names in public!"

"I don't say anything. Nobody talks to me."

"Aha."

Jackie pulls, yanks, and draws off a long strip of wallpaper. Panting slightly, she says, "You don't want them to get in the habit of leaving you out. That's what happened to Mr. Flower."

She scrapes the next strip. "People started leaving Mr. Flower out long ago, maybe when he walked out of school and went fishing. Now they don't even know why they leave him out—it's just a habit they've got into. They tell stories about him behind his back, but they don't talk to Mr. Flower himself. Like, I heard he hasn't spoken to the Stasses in years, since his goat ate their tulips."

"That could be true."

"Sure could. But it's also true the Stasses haven't spoken to him either!"

Jackie pulls and pants. Sweat rolls down her cheeks. "What I'm saying is that everybody's got in the habit of leaving Mr. Russ Flower out of their lives. And we don't want that happening to you."

Thing is, it's already happened.

* * * * * * * * * * * * *14*

*R*ecess Monday is as bad as I knew it would be.

"Neigh!" cries Marigold. "Nei-i-igh!"

I open my mouth to say something, but nothing comes out.

She goes on happily, "And then he sees us. Once he sees us, let me tell you!"

Gathered by the steps, the Court holds its breath. Every eye is trained on Marigold. The ears practically flap.

"He comes for us!" Marigold shrieks. "Teeth bare. Hoofs flying. If my dog Thunder hadn't been there I don't know what—"

I say sharply, "Marigold Stass, you know that isn't true."

Marigold whirls. "Here *she* is, all in one piece! You're one lucky kid, Janet Stone."

Between gloved thumb and first finger Marigold

holds Cliff's Friendship Ring. She was showing it around when she started this horse story. It gleams no brighter than her snapping eyes, or the faces of her Court.

Tough Jessie growls, "So what was it really like, Janet Stone?"

Before I can answer at all Marigold admits, "OK, I exaggerated a bit. He didn't come for us. He was inside the fence. But he took off like—"

Caught up in the story, Marigold hands her Ring to Tunie. She goes on, gesturing and dancing.

"He took off like Superhorse, screaming all the way. Neigh, jump, rear, kick, plunge, buck . . ."

Marigold acts it out and the Court roars laughter. My face flushes hot in the cold air. "And me and Frankie, we just gape like this, we never saw anything like it. And my dog Thunder, he sits down and howls."

I cry, "You spooked Pearl on purpose!" But nobody listens.

"And *she*"—Marigold flings a hand at me—"she sticks to that wild pony like Scotch tape. All she has to do is step off his back, she's bigger'n him"—laughter—"but she hangs on like a rodeo. And they rush round and round . . ."

Marigold rushes off around the yard.

The whole school gets in on this act. All the little kids are running in neighing circles. The yard is in complete uproar, with everyone neighing and laughing. By the steps, Fat Tunie laughs so hard she swallows her bubble gum.

Struggling with the gum, she drops Marigold's Ring on the top step.

One second the Ring winks and sparkles on the top step. Next second it's gone.

Nobody notices because they're laughing too hard.

The bell rings.

Gasping and sobbing laughter, Marigold staggers up to Tunie and holds out her hand.

Tunie looks at her and quits laughing. "What, Marigold?"

"My Ring." Marigold quits laughing.

"Uh . . . I didn't see your Ring."

"I gave it to you." Marigold speaks softly. The Court falls silent.

"Uh . . . well . . ." Tunie pulls her gloves off and shows her ringless fingers. She even turns out her coat pockets. "I don't have it. It isn't here."

Marigold goes white and quiet. The Court holds its breath. Marigold murmurs, "You lost Cliff and my Ring?"

Tunie gulps.

The bell rings again.

Marigold whispers, "See you after school, Tunie Cake."

She pushes between Tunie and me and up the steps.

The Court and the little kids elbow each other up the steps.

Tunie bites her lips. She searches her own pockets again. She squeaks like a caught rabbit, and whimpers. Then she follows the others.

No one looks at me. I pinch the hard, sharp Ring at the bottom of my pocket. I jam it way down to the bottom of the bottom of my pocket. I mount the steps.

No way is this Ring valuable. It's not as if I'm stealing the crown jewels—this came out of some gum machine. This isn't like real stealing at all. This is just getting back a little bit at that mean, mean Marigold.

15

*M*onday afternoon when I walk in the gate, Mr. Flower is milking Rosy. She stands on an old table that leans against the shed, and while he milks, she gobbles a panful of feed. Mr. Flower sits on the table to milk her.

Pearl leans out the shed window. He would love a bite of that feed! Posy sits by Mr. Flower's feet, licking his chops.

I ask, "Is that milk for Posy?"

"Posy and me."

"*You* drink goat milk, Mr. Flower?"

"Well, sure. You drink cow milk."

"That's different."

"Not when they milk it, it's no different."

Actually, I've never seen anyone milk. I know milk comes from cows the way I know the earth circles the sun—books say so.

I move closer. Rosy smells of sweet hay. I touch her warm side, watch her milk foam in the pan.

I say, "Goats are supposed to smell bad."

"Only the buck. Doe smells sweet as clover. You want to milk, Janet?"

"No." I step back.

"Marigold Stass can milk."

"I bet."

"My, yes. That smart Stass kid can change a tire, sew a fine seam, milk a cow. But I bet she's never milked a goat."

Mr. Flower shows me how. "You shut your fist here, keep the milk up in the bag. Now you bump the bag a bit, like a nursing kid would do."

"A baby goat?"

"Right."

"Does Rosy have a kid?"

"Most does have to kid every year or so, or the milk dries up. But my Rosy just milks on and on. Look here now."

You press your fingers down, one by one. Mr. Flower milks best with his good hand, but he can even press his finger stumps. "Practice makes anything perfect, Janet. Here, you try before Rosy finishes that feed up."

I sit on the table, my nose in Rosy's side. I don't really want to grasp her teats, but I do. They are warm and full. I can feel milk in them, like air in balloons. They fit my hands neatly.

"Bump," says Mr. Flower. "Squeeze down. That's how. Don't be scared of it. Lean into it."

Bump, squeeze down. Bump, squeeze down. This is OK. Foaming milk hisses in the pan. I'm really leaning into it when Rosy quits eating. She peers around at me and raises a hind hoof over the pan.

Mr. Flower snatches the pan. "Feed's gone. I'll finish her up. You did good, Janet, first time."

I was enjoying that! Disappointed, I stand back with Posy and watch.

Mr. Flower says, "My Connie always loved her goats."

"Connie?"

"Connie Fisk, she was. From Indian Hill. 'Course, we went to school together." In that one-room school that's now the town office. "Never were friendly there. I liked snakes and spitballs too much. Whoa, Rosy, a minute here . . ."

Rosy stamps small, impatient hoofs. In the shed window, Pearl shakes his snowy mane and blows.

"Then after school I went to work for LeDuc, and Connie made ladies' hats over in Cummington. Clever with her hands, Connie always was. One minute, Rosy. And we forgot each other. There."

Mr. Flower picks up the full pan. Rosy jumps down off the table and nuzzles him. He rubs her ears.

"But every other Saturday was square dancing at

the grange hall. I used to go. I rejoiced to dance! Used to walk across the LeDuc farm and the Bennett farm, and down Main to the Center, ice and snow, hail or rain. And then I'd dance with Connie. Wait till I put this milk away."

Mr. Flower goes in the cabin. Tail high, Posy follows him. Rosy bounds up on her rock pile. In the shed window Pearl nickers, stretching his nose toward the empty feed pan.

I pick it up. It smells of molasses. I hold it up so Pearl can lick at the smell, which is all Rosy left.

Mr. Flower comes back. "I've told you, Janet, the day Pearl works like an ox is the day I give him feed."

"I know. He's just smelling it."

"You couldn't handle him with feed in him! He'd jump over the moon! Ponies get excited."

"You were saying about the dance, Mr. Flower."

Mr. Flower rubs Pearl's forehead and goes on with his story.

"So after-while I commenced walking Connie home after the dance. Indian Hill wasn't exactly on my way. But Connie had changed after school! Put her hair up in a soft brown bun. Got rounder. And she would listen to me! I could talk to Connie.

"So then one winter night, stars bright, snow crunchy, I popped the question. Didn't mean to, it just popped."

I'm hearing an old-fashioned love story! "Connie was your wife!"

"For forty years. And we always had goats around. And we had Stephen."

"Here? Did you live right here for forty years?" With the goats, and Stephen.

"Glory, no! We lived a bit in every part of town. Started out with Connie's folks on Indian Hill. Stayed a bit with my folks in Bug Hollow. Had a farm on Sugar Hill, got burned out. Stayed with my Grandma Cook in your house."

"Our house!"

"That was the old Cook farm. I was born there."

I am really surprised! My mouth just hangs open as he tells me more about our house and its people, and the old days.

* * * * * * * * * * * * **16**

*W*ednesday at recess, Queen Marigold tells her Court, "I made Cliff's birthday cake."

The Court has shrunk. Maybe half the eighth-grade girls cluster around Tunie, over by the gate. Now that she doesn't have to listen to Marigold anymore, Tunie's become a storyteller. I would mosey over there myself, but Marigold is showing snapshots. I hang over Cute Irene's shoulder to see them.

Marigold says, "It was Cliff's nineteenth birthday." *Nineteenth!* Holy trout, what can a man nineteen years old see in Marigold?

She says, "Here's the birthday cake I made. Chocolate. With 'Happy Nineteen Cliff' in sugar sparkles."

I once made a cake from a mix. But this cake is no mix, of course. This is a Marigold Stass cake, made from scratch.

Cute Irene asks, "What did you give him?"

"This." The picture shows Sophie Stass holding out

a blue necktie with red hearts all over it. "I painted the hearts. Freehand."

The Court sighs admiringly.

"Cliff mentioned it matched our Friendship Ring, which of course I couldn't put it on because Tunie stole it."

We all stamp our feet and blow on our fingers. I stamp and blow hardest of all, because Marigold's dumb Ring is heavy in my coat pocket.

I want to get rid of this thing! Why did I ever take it? How could I do such a dumb thing? How do I get rid of it? I've thought of ways—drop it in the snow, leave it in the girls' room—but there are eyes everywhere.

I wish I could write to Maria! Maria is smart. She would surely know some way to give the dratted thing back.

I have to figure this out alone, just me. As usual.

While Marigold scowls we hear Tunie's voice, over by the fence. "So she took the diet pills, see, and she got thin all right. 'Cause those pills had tapeworms in them, see."

Several girls crane their necks, interested. Quickly, Marigold announces, "Here's Cliff! This is Cliff!"

Aha! At last we get to see the mysterious Cliff.

Tough Jessie gets the photograph first. She looks at it eagerly. Then her long face droops, puzzled. She shrugs, and passes the picture to Cute Irene. I lean over Irene's shoulder.

"Cute!" Cute Irene purrs. "He's so cute. . . ." Her purr fades.

The picture shows Frankie Stass smiling up at a plaid work shirt and a hand, which holds the painted necktie. We see Cliff's shirt apparently from the back, neck to waist. Frankie is cute, but Cliff's shirt is not especially exciting.

Jessie growls softly, "Might as well be your brother Andy, far as I can see."

Marigold snatches back the picture. "That's a candid shot, you know. Not posed or anything. Now here's the whole party. Look."

And there they are, a bunch of Stasses grinning greedily at the chocolate cake, with streamers dangling over their heads. But no Cliff.

"That's the best cake I ever made," Marigold proclaims. "The baby thought so, too." She hands out a portrait of Baby Stass all over crushed, smeared cake. "Yech!" says Irene. "Ick!" She has a point.

Turning, I see that several girls have drifted away to hear about Tunie's tapeworms.

I've never really baked a cake or painted a necktie freehand. But I can do something else, something Queen Marigold can't do . . . I don't think.

Deep in my pocket, my fingers grip Marigold's Ring.

I wander off toward Tunie, remembering, smiling into the sunshine.

What would the Court say if I said out loud, right now, "Marigold Stass, I can milk a goat. Can you?"

I milk Rosy often, breathing her sweet rowan hay scent, pressing her warm teats till milk foams in the pan. She doesn't raise a hoof, even after the feed is gone. And afterward she nuzzles me. What would the Court say if I boasted that Rosy Goat liked me?

Yech! They would say. Ick! With their noses in the air.

* * * * * * * * * * * * *17*

$\mathcal{T}$ he bare sponged walls of my room look dismal in lamplight. I imagine them papered with daffodils. Jackie got white wallpaper with daffodils and violets all over. That will be pretty.

I sit up in bed and hear the wind sigh and think about Mr. Flower as a baby being born in this room. The bed must have stood right here—there's no place else for it. Maybe other people were born here, too. I reach for my pad and pencil.

I doodle a daffodil. I doodle trotting hoofs. A pony is trotting past, neck arched, stepping high. He's a circus pony, so I wreathe his neck with flowers and braid more flowers into his mane and tail. Daffodils . . . violets. He is Pearl.

And here I am, poised on tiptoe on his back.

No jeans for me! My short skirt stands straight out. My hair streams and flows. In my raised hands I hold . . . no sponge, mop, or currycomb. Daffodils.

Pearl is snow white. I use dark colors around him, to make him shine.

Now, my spunky little dress. Green, I think, with sugar spangles.

I've lost some weight in this picture, and dyed my hair yellow.

Holy trout! There I sway, tiptoe on Pearl's snowy back, flower-filled hands high. And from one hand red and blue rays shoot off into the dark. I'm disguised as Queen Marigold Stass, complete with Friendship Ring!

I drop the picture. I look suspiciously around my empty room, and draw the Ring from under my pillow.

Held to the light it shines, sparkles, dazzles.

Who can I talk to? Jackie would never understand. I can just see her brown eyes harden! "You *stole* a ring? Take it right back!"

Maria would understand. I imagine her sitting up in bed with me now. (Imaginary people take up very little room.) I ask her, "Maria, what can I do?"

She laughs. "Why, you know, make a big deal? Look the way that girl treats you! She, you know, deserved to lose the thing!"

"I think so too, Maria." (I nod strongly. I wrap my arms around my knees and squeeze them. They think so too. My whole self thinks Marigold deserves to lose this Ring.)

Maria is warming up here. Her black eyes flash and her hair seems to crackle. She growls, "That girl don't know you live in this world with her! She don't know your name is Janet Stone! Time she know, girl, time she know!"

"Wait a sec, Maria—"

"If I was here with you I'd let her know! I'd straighten her hair for her! I'd—"

"Look, Maria. Listen."

The real Maria, back in Holyoke or wherever she is, would not look or listen. She would just go on getting fiercer by the minute. There's no stopping Maria when she gets going.

But I have to handle this my way.

I pick up the pad I had dropped and turn the page. I start drawing.

I draw a girl with straight brown hair in a ponytail, like me. Plump, like me. Her jeans are blue, her shirt is . . . yellow.

It's springtime. She's walking with a friend, shoulders close, almost holding hands.

I draw the friend's hand and arm, and then I wait. I'm not sure what I'm doing.

The friend should have a cloud of black hair and black eyes. She should be plumper than I am. Her name should be Maria.

But now my hand is drawing almost by itself. It draws a tall figure with yellow curls that bounce on slim shoulders. These springy light lines I'm adding here make the curls bounce. A brown shoulder bag bounces on her hip. She wears a white blouse and a flouncy yellow skirt. These two friends smile sideways at each other.

Since it's spring, I put daffodils around their feet. I looked up that poem Mr. Flower didn't recite. The poet, Wordsworth, saw a host of golden daffodils. And after that, any time he liked, he could shut his eyes and see them again. That's just what I do. These drawings I make are like that. I remember things I've seen and sort of think them over again, on paper.

I've seen daffodils, and soft green grass like what I'm drawing now. I've seen friends walking, holding hands and smiling, but I haven't seen these two particular girls. Or have I?

I set the pad up against the headboard of my bed and look closely at the friends. And I see what I've done.

This is what I've gone and done. I've gone and drawn *me* and snooty Marigold Stass like friends!

I grab the pad and rip off the sheet. I commence to crumple it up. I want to rip it up, to throw it in the waste can in a hundred pieces.

I stop. What with all those fancy daffodils, and the curls that really bounce, it's too good to throw out. Sometime I might want to copy parts of it for some other picture.

I smooth out the paper and tuck it back in the pad, toward the end, where I won't have to see it.

I still don't know what to do about the Ring.

* * * * * * * * * * * * * * *18*

*W*hen crows call in the woods, Mr. Flower's eyes gleam. He calls, "Come on, Janet Stone! Sugaring time!"

He carries a pile of pails. I carry a sack of jingly things. We leave Pearl and Rosy looking over the fence and go into the woods. Posy squeezes through the fence and follows us, tail twitching high.

Here the snow is still deep, soft, and sticky. We stop at the first old maple tree, and Mr. Flower sets the pails down.

"You hand me the tools," he says, "I'll do the job. First, the bit."

Bit? In the sack of jingly things I find a bunch of small, silvery troughs, a hammer, and a sort of screwdriver with a turning handle. I hand him that.

Mr. Flower sets the point into the rough bark and turns the handle. The point sinks in. A clear liquid bleeds around the point and spills down the bark.

"Perfect timing!" he says happily. "Crows always tell you right."

"Mr. Flower, what is that stuff?"

"That stuff is your maple sap, Janet. It makes pancake syrup, and sugar for Arthur. Give me a trough and the hammer."

Posy stretches up to lick the dripping sap. I hand Mr. Flower his tools and lick a drop of sap off my finger. It tastes very faintly sweet.

Mr. Flower sets the point of the trough in the wet hole and hammers it in. He hangs a pail from the trough and adds a roof over the pail. The sap goes ping! ping! in the pail.

"That's it. Come on, come on!" Rejoicing, Mr. Flower gallops to the next big tree. "It'll freeze tonight. Just what you want. Warm day, cold night. Sap will flow out like money!"

"Doesn't it hurt the tree?"

"Not a bit. We just hang one pail per tree. Tree can handle that."

"What about when the pail fills up?"

"We boil the sap."

"Where?"

"Folks who tap a lot of trees have a sugarhouse to boil in. My cabin is Grandma Cook's old sugarhouse. I do my sap in there. Quick, Janet, the trough!"

The woods air smells fresh. Crows call and flap. A

squirrel lollops over snow. Posy looks after him, but doesn't follow. Posy's an old cat—he's chased enough squirrels. Wading on to the next tree, I step in Mr. Flower's limping track.

"You want to look sharp here, Janet, like your pal Marigold Stass. Step lively now, or I'll hire—"

"No you won't, Mr. Flower." I'm pretty sure.

"Huh?"

"You won't hire Marigold Stass."

"Hm. Well, you're right about that. That kid is too smart for me." He goes to work on the tree. "This is where my Granda Cook taught me to work."

"Right here?"

"On these very same trees. This was Granda's sugar bush. He would bring three-four of us grandkids out here, sugar time, and he'd keep us hopping! We learned how to work, let me tell you! The Indians taught the settlers how to sugar, and Granda's granda taught him, and glory, did he teach us kids!"

Two trees later Mr. Flower says, "Tell you what happened one time. We came out early, sun just up. And over behind that tree there a gray thing jumped up out of the snow. It said, 'Whuff whuff,' and it took off leaping, like flying, with a white tail waving like a flag. Know what that was?"

"No. What?"

"Us kids didn't know. We were scared. Granda said

it was the first deer he'd seen in Winterfield. Said the wildlife was commencing to move down from the north. Nothing to what it is now, of course!"

I think about that. At the next tree I ask, "Is there wildlife here now?"

"I should say! Now the old farms are mostly gone, the woods are growing back. The new people stay in their new houses—they don't go out back. So the wildlife has the run of the woods."

I'm looking around me now! "What sort of wildlife is out here?"

Mr. Flower shrugs. "Beaver. Bear. I remember one spring morning when we lived at your house, Stephen brought a newborn fawn into the kitchen. Said, 'This is our new pet. He can drink goat milk.' Stephen was always wild for pets."

"Did you keep the fawn?"

"Glory, no! Connie chased Stephen and that fawn right back to where it came from. Mama Doe was running around out there bleating for her baby. You can bet that was one happy reunion!"

So Stephen was wild for pets. Pearl is my pet. I bet he's waiting for me now, watching for me over the fence. When he sees me he will nicker, like saying hi. And when I come up to him he will lay his head on my shoulder. He does that now.

His chin is hard and heavy, but I never push him off.

Daylight begins to sink into snow. Shadows creep among the trees like the wildlife Mr. Flower tells of. I'm glad when he says, "That's it. Let's get back to feed and water before dark. Quick now, Janet, like Marigold Stass."

* * * * * * * * * * * * *19*

$\mathcal{M}$y wallpaper is up! Jackie and I pant and sweat and admire the bright walls covered with little violets and daffodils.

"Good thing it's a small room," Jackie sighs.

"Looks bigger now."

"Aha, yes. The tiny print makes it seem bigger."

We glance around, beaming. I'm about to say, "Cocoa break?" when Jackie hauls a new tool out of her apron pocket.

I cry, "Not more work!"

"Just a bit more. You roll the seams smooth-smooth with this. Oddly enough, it's called a seam roller." It's a wheel on a handle. "I'll trim the edges. Surely you didn't expect to leave them ragged!"

I don't need to answer that.

I commence rolling seams smooth-smooth. It's not hard work. Nothing compared with what we've been doing. Jackie climbs on our workbench. She presses her putty knife against the top of the paper and cuts off the overlap with her razor knife. Her long braid swings back and forth as she works.

After a tired silence Jackie asks, "So how is your friend Pearl doing?"

"Pearl's great. Looks great, acts great, eats great." And I'm beginning to love him.

"That fat look he had was just hair, wasn't it?"

"Winter coat. And dirt. Under that he was just bones. He's filled out now."

"Aha. And how is Mr. Russell Flower?"

"Jackie, I forgot to tell you!" I quit rolling to look up at her. "Mr. Flower was born here!"

"In this house?"

"In this room!"

"His family owned this place?"

"His grandma Cook owned it. She planted daffodils by the porch."

"Aha. We'll be seeing them soon."

"You think they're still there?"

"Daffodils go on forever. Roll, Jannie!"

I go back to work. "You think anybody else was born in this room, Jackie?"

"I bet. Bet folks died in it, too."

I glance around my room. Drifting clouds throw ghostly shadows. "If I think like that it doesn't feel like *my* room."

"It's yours while you're in it. Keep rolling."

I roll. "Jackie, Mr. Flower says we've got wildlife out back."

"Aha! I love to meet wild animals. They're like men from Mars."

"Huh?"

"They live in their own world, alongside our world. Gives you a whole new outlook."

I'm living in my own world, alongside Jackie's world. My hand slips into my pocket and fingers the Ring. Could I say right now, "Jackie, I have a friend who stole a Ring. What should she do?"

I could not. Jackie would know right off. Her eyes would go harder than this dratted Ring burning my fingers.

Could I maybe just drop the thing in the trash and walk away humming?

I wish I could! But this Ring is almost like a live thing, a little animal crouched in my pocket. It's got *me* wrapped up in it, and Marigold, and Tunie, and this Cliff guy nobody's ever seen. It's not worth fifty cents, but it weighs in my pocket like a diamond. I just couldn't throw it away.

* * * * * * * * * * * 20

*M*ost every day I ride Pearl. We cross Hungry Hollow Road and take a trail into the woods. It meets a dirt road that leads along behind the Hungry Hollow houses.

Mr. Flower calls this Old King's Road. He says the first Winterfield settlers called it the King's Highway. Massachusetts belonged to England back then. The settlers trudged out here with their oxcarts full of furniture and built houses. All that's left of those houses now are cellar holes in the woods. "They went on west," Mr. Flower says. "But first they cleared miles of pasture here. Hundreds of sheep grazed along the King's Highway." Now it's all woods.

Our Hungry Hollow Road was where the very first settler settled. One winter he went fifteen miles to Northampton for supplies. It snowed so hard he couldn't come back, and his hungry family ate their dog. Not even Mr. Flower knows for sure where their house stood, but it was somewhere in Hungry Hollow.

"History or legend," Jackie says, "fact or fiction, Russ Flower tells a good story!"

The snow is melting in the woods, and Pearl steps out easily. This is OK. We trot as far as the curve before the Stass house. There I draw rein.

The big peeling-white Stass house has chicken coops out back that spill clucking hens all over the yard. Rabbits hunch in hutches. Most days diapers blow, sag, and freeze on the line. Indoors, most days, the TV booms and doors slam. Kids may rush out any minute. The big black dog with a growl like thunder guards everything. Going by Stass, Pearl pricks his ears and walks tensely. Going by Stass, I keep a tight hand on the reins.

ONE tight hand! I ride one-hand now, guiding Pearl with a graceful sway left or right. Most of the time we move like a team.

But on this bright Saturday morning we walk slowly around the bend into the midst of the Stasses.

They're all out here in the woods. There's Mr. and Mrs., Baby, little Frankie, Sophie, Andy, two older ones I don't know, Marigold, and a young man with red hair. No Stass has red hair. Red must be hired help.

They are stringing green hoses from tree to tree. Mr. Flower told me that's the modern way to tap maple trees. It saves a lot of hauling.

The black dog, Thunder, explodes out of snow and rushes us.

Pearl shies, rears, and jumps in circles. Calming him takes a while. Then I see all the Stasses staring at us. Red holds Thunder's collar. Thunder digs snow and climbs air to get at us.

Beside Red, Marigold wears deep purple eyelids, crooked lipstick, and one dangling earring. Hammer in hand, she stares at us as if she never saw us before.

Pearl shudders. I pat his neck and prickle and blush, and look for a way out. I'd love to ride straight through all these staring Stasses! But there are hoses snaking all around to trip Pearl, and a camera for him to step on, and Baby Stass toddling right in our way. We'd best turn around like this and—

"Hey, you!" Mr. Stass roars. "Wait up."

I wheel Pearl back to face him. He lumbers up to us. "That Flower's old pony from the auction?"

I nod.

"Don't look the same."

I gulp. "We . . . we've been working with him."

"You done a good job." Mr. Stass gives Pearl a friendly whack on the shoulder. Pearl shies and shudders. "Good thing you don't have far to fall! Don't let him step on this here hose."

"I won't."

"Go through here."

"I will."

A voice calls, "Hey Jannie! Jannie!" Frankie runs up.

"Can I have a ride, huh?"

Marigold has boasted that she knitted Frankie's pull-down cap. Blond hair spills from under it. Eager blue eyes look up. "Can I?"

The way Pearl is shivering, I'm not sure what he'll do. But Frankie is the first person in Winterfield to call me Jannie. It melts me. I hear myself say, "Sure, Frankie."

Mr. Stass says, "Just to Main Road and back. We got work cut out here."

Marigold snorts.

I step off Pearl. "Say hi to Pearl first, Frankie. Let him smell your hand."

Pearl smells Frankie all over. He mumbles, and stops shivering.

"He likes me, he likes me!" Frankie rejoices.

I hoist him up. He sits loose and easy, with a light grip on Pearl's mane.

"You ride before, Frankie?"

"Yeah, I ride Uncle Joe's workhorses." I should have guessed! Frankie is a Stass.

I lead Pearl the way Mr. Stass pointed out. Marigold doesn't glance our way, but Red's warm brown eyes smile at us.

Behind us I hear panting, and fast-thudding paws. The great black dog bounds past us, spattering snow.

Pearl stiffens and throws up his head.

Frankie pats his neck. "It's OK, Pearl," he says. "You're my friend, so you're Thunder's friend."

Pearl seems to believe this. He nods and walks on.

Frankie tells me, "I call Thunder 'Thunder' because he growls like thunder."

"I know!"

"Good old Pearl," says Frankie, still patting. "Next time we ride I'll bring you some maple sugar."

$\mathcal{T}$his drawing won't get color. It's soft pencil, gray and black and white. I rub with the pencil to make shadows and shaded lines. You don't need color every time.

I draw a bare maple tree, so huge and old it carries two sap buckets. The tree rears up and reaches out. Branches . . . branches . . . I rub deep shadows into the bark.

Under the tree stands a stooped old man with a cap drawn down over his face. He holds a pail in one mittened hand. A boy reaches to take the pail.

The boy smiles up at the old man. He looks a bit like Frankie Stass, but older. Maybe he's ten.

Arthur Flower is ten.

I chew the pencil.

I've drawn Mr. Flower and Arthur. They are tapping maple trees in the woods where Granda Cook taught Russ Flower to work.

Mr. Flower would love to teach Arthur to work!

This is a sad picture because Mr. Flower and Arthur will never sugar together. Arthur only comes to Winterfield when the apple tree blooms, and maple sugaring is over then.

Color would help the sadness. Blue shadows, pink snow like at sunset, would cheer up the picture.

But I'm going to leave it sad, like it really is.

*T*hursday recess, Queen Marigold says, "I don't dare tell Cliff Tunie stole the Ring."

The Court sighs. Everyone is tired of hearing about this Ring. Deep in my coat pocket, I pinch it.

Where snow has melted by the fence Tunie's new Court jumps rope. Fat Tunie doesn't jump. She swings one end, pops gum, and leads the chant.

> *"Hey, hey, I had a good jump on my Ring!*
> *Hey, hey, a Ring's a thing makes you sing!*
> *A Ring you send,*
> *A Ring you lend,*
> *A Ring you keep for a friend, hey!"*

I bet Tunie made that up.

Tough Jessie says, "Marigold, you want to forget this rattling Ring. Tunie didn't steal it, no more than I did. Why don't you blame Janet Stone? She was there too."

I freeze. Here it comes. Standing rigid, I roll the Ring deep in my coat pocket. I can't breathe.

Marigold's blue eyes sharpen. She frowns.

Jessie barks, "Oh come on! You think Stuck-up Janet's got your Ring? Next thing you'll say Irene did it!"

Nervously, Irene pats her curls.

I may just throw up.

Marigold's eyes hold me. I look back at her and roll the Ring deep, deep in my coat pocket.

Tough Jessie growls, "You say that word *Ring* once more, Marigold, and I'll go jump rope."

Marigold shrugs and turns away. I breathe.

Marigold picks a little radio off the steps. "Cliff lent me this," she says, "so we can dance."

She turns it on. Rock music hammers. She turns it up. Rock music roars. Marigold dances.

Quick-quick, I dance too. Graceful Marigold, smirking Irene, jerky Jessie dance past. The yard swings around. The rock music drowns out Tunie's chant.

> *"A Ring you send,*
> *A Ring you lend,*
> *A Ring you keep for a friend, hey."*

I wonder, what's that Jessie said about "Stuck-up Janet"? She can't mean *me*, surely!

* * * * * * * * * * * *23*

*B*efore each ride I comb and brush Pearl's coat. Then after the ride, Mr. Flower and I clean pebbles and gravel out of Pearl's hoofs. I used to think all horses wore iron shoes, but Mr. Flower says a pony ridden on dirt roads doesn't need shoes— he just needs his hoofs cleaned every time.

When we ride in this evening Mr. Flower is milking Rosy on the table. Posy waits beside him, licking his chops. By myself I crosstie Pearl to the outside shed wall. By myself I crouch, lift each small, dirty hoof, and scrape it clean. Pearl stands still. He trusts me.

He trusts me, but he really likes Frankie Stass! Maybe three times a week we just happen to meet Frankie and Thunder on Old King's Road. I help Frankie mount Pearl, and the three of them gallop away.

I amble along the muddy road and listen to new birds call, and squirrels chatter among small, new leaves. It's lonesome. Lonesomeness floats away from me into the woods, and new thoughts float in. I wonder if hidden animals watch me pass. I wonder if the settlers' oxen grazed under these old beech trees, long ago.

After Frankie rides, these little hoofs need cleaning!

Mr. Flower comes over to see how I do hoofs by myself. "Good," he says. "Nice. Marigold Stass could do no better. Have a sugar."

I stand up and accept a tiny square of golden maple sugar.

"Rejoices you, don't it? That will rejoice Arthur, too. Pearl, you rejoice too." Mr. Flower doesn't often give Pearl treats. He says treats teach a pony to nip your hand. But we can't very well rejoice like this without sharing! Rosy trots up and rejoices, too. Then she dances away to bully her swinging tire.

"Mr. Flower," I say, "there's daffodils coming up in our yard."

"Yep. Grandma Cook planted those."

"Did you own our house?" Jackie and I have been wondering if Mr. Flower minds our living there.

"Never did. I owned a share of that house, along with my cousins. I sold my share for Stephen."

"What do you mean, for Stephen?"

"Well, see, Stephen was bright. He liked school. My Connie went to work cooking at the Route Nine Diner so he could go to college."

"My mom worked her way through college." I've heard a lot about that.

"Stephen worked, sure enough. But this was one high-class college we're talking about. And law school. And Connie got sick and died. So I sold my share of the Cook farm so Stephen could finish up."

"Oh." I see.

I free Pearl from the crossties. He turns and rests his hard chin on my shoulder. I lift strands of his silky mane in my fingers. "Look, Mr. Flower. Pearl is pretty now."

"Arthur will rejoice to see him. Tomorrow we commence yard cleaning for Arthur."

"What! So soon?"

"Look at the apple tree."

Late sunshine glows on the apple branches. On every twig green buds swell, ready to burst. The apple tree is getting ready to bloom!

And Mr. Flower is getting ready for Arthur.

And I must get ready, right now, to say good-bye to Pearl. Just as we've really made friends, Pearl will go away to Castlebridge with Arthur. I may never see him again!

His heavy chin digs into my shoulder, but I don't push him off.

"Holy trout," I say, "I didn't know it was spring!"

"Crept up on you," says Mr. Flower.

* * * * * * * * * * * * *24*

*J*ackie cries, "Watch it!"

Too late. Just for one minute I thought about something else, and the cloth ran right off the sewing machine. The machine clacks away at nothing, tangling its threads.

"The pedal, Jannie! Take your foot off the pedal."

That's better. Silence. Hopefully I ask, "Is it ruined?"

"No, of course it isn't ruined. And you could fix it if it was."

I groan. That's the thing about sewing. You can't just ruin it, say, "Too bad," and walk off. You can always fix it, and fixing is harder than sewing.

Jackie whips the yellow-spangled curtain material off the sewing table. She shakes it, studies it, turns it, pats it down like a pet. "No harm done," she says. "But those threads are well tangled."

Yech! I poke my nose down in the machine. Looks

like I'll have to dig the bobbin out and thread it again. Ick!

I ask, "Why do we have to make curtains anyhow? They've got them all made in the store."

"Not that match your wallpaper."

Drat the wallpaper! "Maybe it would be easier sewing by hand."

"Aha. Jannie, you're getting discouraged."

No kidding! My back aches, my eyes ache, I'm yellow-speck dizzy. Oh, to be riding Pearl down Old King's Road right now!

"Let me fix it." Jackie takes my place and bends into the machine. Her brown braid swings down her shoulder. "Tsk tsk," she says. "You must have been thinking about something else."

Actually, I was thinking about the Ring in my pocket. I was searching for some way to get it back to Marigold without anyone suspecting. But I can't very well say that.

I say, "I was thinking about Mr. Flower."

"Aha. What about him?"

"Um, I was thinking how excited he is about Arthur coming. He's wild about that Arthur. I was wondering if my Grandpa Stone was that wild about me."

"Oh, Jannie!" Jackie quits fussing with the bobbin. She looks up at me sadly. If I didn't know Jackie I would think she might cry. She flips her braid back and says, "Jannie, my father never met you."

"Never once?"

"Never once. He lived in San Francisco. We lived in Massachusetts. Nobody had money to travel."

"And how about my other grandpa?"

"You know your dad had no family."

I wander off to the window and look out at the new spring leaves. Now all I see from my window is leaves.

I've always wished I had uncles, aunts, cousins. Relatives. Just Jackie and me is lonesome! I used to envy Maria her wild brothers. Now I sort of envy Marigold her noisy family.

I think out loud, "I wish I could adopt Mr. Flower for my grandpa."

I wonder, could I talk to Mr. Flower about this Ring?

Jackie bends to the sewing machine. She says, "Grandpas aren't all that great. They tell the same old stories over and over, and you have to listen politely."

"You loved your grandpa," I remind her.

"Aha! Yes I did. But I didn't love hearing those stories every day!"

Mr. Flower might know how to handle this Ring thing. I bet he might even understand it.

* * * * * * * * * * * 25

*P*earl and I amble down Old King's Road. We move happily together. I love the thunk of Pearl's small hoofs on moss. I love the flop of his fluffy mane. Even though I'm getting seriously too big for Pearl, I will miss our rides when Arthur takes him away.

I ride loosely, looking around, hoping to see wildlife. Some wild thing might look at me out of any leafy shadow. We would look at each other from our different worlds. It would be like meeting a man from Mars.

Pearl stumbles. Something is stuck in his right hoof.

"Whoa." I slide the short way to earth and drop Pearl's reins under his nose. Mr. Flower has taught him to stand still like that, for maybe a minute. I kneel in moss and pick up the hoof.

Pearl snorts and jerks up his head. I catch hold of the reins.

A young man is strolling toward us. He wears work clothes. He has red hair and brown eyes.

He is Red, who works for Mr. Stass.

I blush and prickle. I would rather see a wild thing than a person I may have to talk to! I stand up.

Red nods and smiles. He asks, "Trouble?"

"Oh, no! No trouble."

"You were looking at his hoof."

"Um, I thought he had a stone in it."

"Let me look." And before I can speak, before Pearl can lay his ears back, Red kneels and picks up his hoof. I hang on to those reins!

Red says, "Yep." And before we know what he's doing he whips out a jackknife and scrapes a pebble out of Pearl's hoof. "See this? These jokers can do a job." He throws the pebble away and stands up. "This is old Mr. Flower's pony, right?"

"Right."

"And you're Janet Stone. Your mom teaches shop."

"Right."

"Mind if I call you Jannie?"

"Oh! Sure!" I prickle like crazy.

"I'm Cliff LeDuc."

Cliff? He's Cliff?

"I'm going to work at the Stasses'. You walk along with me, see how the hoof does."

Holy trout! This is Marigold's famous boyfriend, Cliff! But I saw him once working with Marigold, and they didn't seem especially romantic.

I turn Pearl around. The three of us walk together like friends.

Cliff asks, "How's he doing?"

"Um, I think he's better." In fact, Pearl walks just fine.

"Jannie, what does old Mr. Flower want with a pony like this?"

"He's going to give him to his grandson, Arthur."

"His grandson lives in the city. Where will they keep a pony?"

"I don't know."

"Well, Jannie, you've done a great job on him."

"Thanks." Prickle.

"You must be a nice girl."

Blush!

"I bet you've learned a lot, helping Mr. Flower."

"Um, yes."

"I like to know how to do things. That's why I work for Mr. Stass. I've learned a lot there."

It's now or never. I take a deep, strong breath. Bravely I say, "I've heard Marigold Stass mention you, Cliff."

"Marigold's a good kid. The Stasses know how to raise good kids."

"She said she made your birthday cake."

"Yep. They gave me a real surprise party. Marigold made the cake, Sophie made paper flowers, Frankie streamed the streamers, Andy bought pop. They were great."

I take another deep breath. "Marigold said she painted a tie for you."

"Yep. I've got it at the back of my closet."

"The back of your closet?"

"Well, Jannie, it's got red hearts all over it! Maybe I'll wear it next year, Valentine's Day."

Inside me, a sort of caged bird opens its wings.

"Here's your turnoff, Jannie. Have Mr. Flower check that hoof."

The hoof's just fine. "Cliff, wait a sec!"

Cliff waits.

I swallow, hard. Now we come to *it*. "What about the Ring?"

"Ring?"

"You . . . gave Marigold a Ring? With a red stone?"

Cliff frowns, thinking. "Oh! You mean the gum-machine ring at the mall. We were all hanging out there one night. I gave the ring to Sophie, and I guess she traded it to Marigold."

"I'm talking about this Ring." I pick it out of my pocket and show it to Cliff, all gleaming.

"That's right."

Inside me, the caged bird steps out of his cage.

"Marigold said she changed a tire for you one night."

"Yep. I turned my ankle chasing Frankie around in the dark."

"Frankie! Frankie was there?"

"Of course. The Stasses do everything together, Jannie. Everything. That's their recipe for a good family life. Always together."

"Aha!" Doesn't sound to me like a recipe for a good romance!

"Nice to meet you, Jannie."

"Um, me too." I'll say!

Cliff strolls on toward the Stass place. I climb onto Pearl. We canter up the trail to Hungry Hollow Road.

Inside me, the uncaged bird claps his wings and flies.

I've got Marigold where I want her!

Marigold Stass is through, finished!

Just wait till the Court hears about this!

Cantering through green spring woods, I laugh aloud.

* * * * * * * * * * * * *26*

"*M*r. Flower!" I shout, galloping into the yard. "Mr. Flower!"

He hobbles out of the shed as fast as he can, and I'm sorry I shouted.

"It's OK," I call, swinging down before Pearl even stops all the way. "Nothing bad happened."

"So what's the commotion?"

I show him the Ring.

"A gum-machine Ring?" He takes it in his gnarled fingers. "You found it?"

"Um, a . . . friend of mine stole it."

Mr. Flower gives me a sideways look. "You said nothing bad happened."

"Well, see, it happened a time back."

"You're all-fired excited about something that happened a time back."

"You see . . ." I tell him how my friend Maria

snatched the Ring, and Marigold blamed Fat Tunie. And of course I had to keep Maria's secret.

"Sounds kind of hard on Fat Tunie," Mr. Flower remarks.

"But how about Maria!"

I tell how I just met Cliff, and the rest of the story. "I figure Marigold deserved to be stolen from, after fooling us all about her boyfriend!"

Mr. Flower chuckles. Then he frowns. He's looking at me very sharply over the shining Ring. I'm not at all sure he believes the Maria story.

Finally he asks, "What are you going to do about it?"

"I don't know. That's what I want to ask you."

Pearl rests his chin on my shoulder. I pat his nose. Mr. Flower twirls the Ring in the sunlight, watching it glow.

"If it was me," he says, "I'd leave this shiny thing on a bush for Marigold Stass to find."

"I never thought of that!" It wouldn't even have to be at school. She could find it on her way home, beside Hungry Hollow Road.

"And I'd keep quiet about the boyfriend business."

"Keep quiet!" How can I keep quiet when I'm ready to burst! And why should I?

Mr. Flower nods and hands me the Ring back. "Folks get upset having their secrets told. Miss Marigold will forget about this here Ring someday. But she'd never never forget if you told the kids there wasn't any boyfriend! Glory hallelujah, she'd hold that against you when she was ninety! She wouldn't ask you to her ninety-fifth birthday party because of that! So if you want to get to be friends, ever, just keep it secret."

I gulp. Mr. Flower grins at my disappointed face. "You might whisper just to Marigold, 'All is discovered.' That would set her down right!"

I shake my head. "Not far enough, Mr. Flower."

"And what about friend Maria, and this famous Ring? Seems to me the score's even."

Mr. Flower twinkles at me. Then he says sternly, "Now brush Pearl down good, Janet. We want him tip-top shape for Arthur, Sunday."

And I see the apple tree's in bloom, all over blossoms as white as Pearl.

"I want you here Sunday," Mr. Flower says. "Old Pearl's a handful, and so is Arthur."

Pearl breathes on me and rubs his forehead against my shoulder. I have helped make him warm and glossy and friendly, and Sunday he'll go away. I don't think I can stand Sunday.

* * * * * * * * * * * *27*

*M*r. Flower throws up his head. His beard and eyebrows twitch. Out on Main Road a car has turned onto Hungry Hollow Road.

Mr. Flower cries, "That's Arthur!"

He hugs himself to hold in his excitement, but it gleams around him like a halo.

Under the blooming apple trees I stand between Pearl and Rosy, one hand on each warm, white neck. I prickle and blush. Rosy and Pearl perk ears and swish tails. We all watch nervously as the great, gleaming car dips around the bend and stops at the gate.

Mr. Flower squeaks, "Arthur!" and hobbles to the gate.

Stephen leaps out the driver's side and strides to shake Mr. Flower's hand. Stephen is dark, slender, elegant in a light suit and yellow tie. His wavy brown hair lifts on a breeze, his brown eyes smile.

Mrs. Flower unfolds herself gingerly from the car. Fair and slender, she wears a beige dress with a yellow scarf. Her high heels teeter in mud. When Mr. Flower hobbles to hug her, she steps quickly away.

The small white face in the backseat is Arthur.

This pale, skinny little kid creeps out into Mr. Flower's bear hug and hangs there, limp. I thought Arthur the Great would wear a halo, but the halo is on Mr. Flower. I've heard of sorrow breaking hearts. If joy can break a heart, Mr. Flower's heart is in danger of cracking.

Mrs. Flower advances slowly into the yard. She folds her arms and bites her lips, looking about her. Right away I know something about Mrs. Flower: She's prickling.

She doesn't want to be here. Winterfield is Stephen's home ground, not hers. She doesn't like Winterfield, she doesn't like Mr. Flower, and she wishes she were someplace else, someplace she understands, like Castlebridge.

"Father Flower!" she calls shrilly. "That old apple tree will fall on you one of these days! I've told you before."

Her prickly eye lights on me. I shrink back behind

Pearl. Her eye lights on Pearl. "Father Flower!" she calls. "Why are you keeping a *horse*? The *goat* was bad enough!"

Mr. Flower says, "Arthur, look at this." He swings Arthur around toward us. "See that bee-oo-tiful pony there?"

Arthur sees. Mr. Flower waits in vain for him to rejoice.

Mr. Flower declares, "Arthur. That wonderful pony is *yours*."

Arthur goes paler than before. He tries to back off, but Mr. Flower grips him by the shoulders.

Mrs. Flower whirls. "Oh, Father Flower! This is too much! You know very well we can't keep a *pony* in *town*! Stephen, explain to your father. It's beyond me."

She turns her back and stumps off to inspect the yard. Stab, stab, go her heels in the new-raked earth. She would just love to climb into that big shiny car and whoosh right back to civilized Castlebridge, which is her world.

Arthur hangs limply in Mr. Flower's grip and stares at Pearl with horrified eyes. I know he feels just the same as Mrs. Flower.

Stephen sighs. "Father, our yard is ten feet square. There's no shed—"

"Glory, you can rent a stall somewheres."

"And you see, Father, there's no time. Arthur's got school and piano and figure skating and computer—"

"No time for a *pony*? Stephen! You remember LeDuc's old donkey was your best friend? Violet, they called him. You remember how you dolled him up for the Fourth of July parade?"

Stephen blushes deep red down to his necktie. I bet he prickles, too.

"You want your son to doll up his best friend too, right?"

Stephen opens his mouth, but no words come out.

Mr. Flower turns back to Arthur. "Arthur," he says firmly, "come here and meet your new pony. His name is Pearl."

He drags Arthur under Pearl's nose.

Mrs. Flower calls from the raspberry patch, "Stephen! That beast may bite!"

She's right. Under my hand Pearl's neck tenses. His ears fold back. His teeth gleam yellow. Arthur smells of fear. His fear frightens Pearl.

Mr. Flower is too excited to notice this. "Look, Arthur! When I was ten I'd have given all my teeth for a gorgeous pony like this! Your father would have, too. He always loved his pets." Mr. Flower swings Arthur up on Pearl's back.

Pearl jerks, shudders, and whisks his tail.

Arthur whines, "Grandpa, let me off!"

Mr. Flower beams at frightened Pearl and terrified Arthur. He just doesn't see them as they really are. All he sees is his dream come true—his grandson on beautiful Pearl.

Mr. Flower doesn't dream that Arthur is nothing like him. Arthur would much rather play Nintendo than ride Pearl. To Arthur, Pearl isn't beautiful, he's dangerous. And to Pearl, Arthur isn't the world's greatest kid, he's a stranger who stinks of fear. And fear means that there is something to fear.

Arthur whimpers.

"It's fine," Mr. Flower assures him. "I'm holding the halter." And he is, but loosely.

From the garden plot Mrs. Flower wails, "Stephen! Your father's been spading again! He shouldn't work like this at his age. Tell him what we decided."

Stephen mutters, "Not right now, dear." Watching Arthur on Pearl, his brown eyes turn cloudy.

Mrs. Flower doesn't hear, or doesn't want to hear. She calls, "Stephen! Tell Father Flower what I told you!"

Stephen heaves a great sigh. Holy trout, I'm sorry for Stephen! He's stuck in the middle between two people who really don't like each other, and he likes them both. He wants to see both of them happy, and he can't.

"Father," he says, still watching Arthur on Pearl. "We want you to come live in Castlebridge."

Mr. Flower looks at him. "With you and Arthur?"

"Around the corner, in the new senior citizen condominium."

Mr. Flower turns back to Arthur. He says, "Show Pearl how much you like him. Relax. Pat his neck."

Desperately, Stephen says, "Father, we've signed you up for a condo—"

Mr. Flower whirls on Stephen. He growls like Frankie Stass's Thunder. A red tide of rage floods his face. He shakes, and spits when he talks.

Mr. Flower has turned into a werewolf! Or rather, he's turned into the Mad Hermit of Winterfield kids talk of. I've never seen him like this, and neither has Pearl.

He shouts, "You dithering ninny! You slobbering wimp! This is my home, right here!"

"Father—"

"How dare you sign me up! You can't sign me up for no condo, nor Paree France, nor heaven neither! I'm signed up here till I unsign—me, not you!"

Pearl shies. The halter rips from Mr. Flower's hand. Mrs. Flower shrieks, "Stephen!"

Pearl takes off at a dead gallop.

Arthur hangs on for all he's worth, yelling, "Ee! Ee! Ee!"

Rosy bounds up on her rock pile and watches the action from safe on high.

Mane and tail streaming, Pearl gallumphs past the raspberries, past the garden, behind the cabin.

Side by side, Mr. Flower and I watch Pearl stampede. There's no way to stop him. I glance out the corner of my eye and see Mr. Flower's shoulders collapsed in a stoop, his face crumpled, and, holy trout, a tear sliding down his cheek.

I'm sorry for Mr. Flower. The Stephen Flowers will never come back here after this!

I'm sorry for dumb Arthur, too. It's not his fault he's dumb. And I know so well how he feels! Pearl ran away with me once, and I was bigger than Arthur. My feet could almost touch the snow.

Pearl and Arthur gallop back into sight. "Ee! Ee! Ee!"

Mrs. Flower cries, "Stephen! Catch the beast!"

But this is an order Stephen can't obey.

Mr. Flower steps forward, but not even he can control Pearl right now.

"Ee! Ee! Ee!"

Pearl has had about enough of this screeching, clinging load on his back. At the raspberry patch he pauses, whirls in a circle, dances on his hind legs. He comes down thump! on his front legs, tosses his croup in the air, and hurls Arthur high.

"Ee! Ee! Ee!"

Pearl shakes his mane and gallops off, rejoicing.

Falling takes Arthur's breath away. Silent, he thuds into the raspberry thorns.

* * * * * * * * * * * *28*

*M*onday morning I leave early for school. I've always gone later so as not to see Marigold Stass on the road. Today I'm out to catch her.

Low, dark smoke drifts out of Mr. Flower's stovepipe and hangs in the yard like fog. Posy sits sadly in the shed window, dangling his limp tail down the wall. I look the other way and hurry on by.

I round the bend. Maybe Marigold's gone already. Maybe she's late. Maybe there's someone with her for a change. Maybe—

There she goes, nose high, shoulder bag swinging. Her yellow curls bounce on her shoulders.

There goes Marigold Stass, who fooled everybody and made me look dumb and made me steal her stupid gum-machine ring and then have to worry about it.

Marigold doesn't know it, but justice is finally trotting up behind her. Me. At last, disaster is finally going to hit the wonderful world of Marigold Stass. Me.

I take a deep, strong breath and shout, "Hey, you! You, Marigold Stass!"

She wheels. She sees me, but she doesn't believe I shouted that. She looks around for somebody else, somebody more important. Poor Marigold is in for a real shock!

"It's me," I yell. "Me, Janet Stone. Wait up, Marigold Stass!"

Marigold's mouth drops wide open. She waits. I trot up to her.

"Marigold, I want for you to be the first to know."

"To know what?"

"I met somebody the other day on Old King's Road. Red hair. Just turned nineteen. Thought I'd seen him somewhere before, and I had."

Marigold looks at me the way Pearl used to. Suspicious. I say, "Friendly, isn't he? You know who."

Marigold looks the way Pearl used to when he thought about taking a good bite out of my hand.

"He mentioned you, Marigold. Called you a good kid. His exact words were, 'The Stasses know how to raise good kids.' And, 'The Stasses do everything together.' Hard to start up a romance with family all around. Right, Marigold?"

Marigold turns red. She turns white. She tosses her hair and stamps her foot, just like Pearl. She snarls, "OK, so I made up a good story."

"Good story! You kept those poor kids holding their breath with that story!"

"What poor kids?"

"Fat Tunie! Tough Jessie! Cute Irene!"

Marigold steps in real close. She whispers in my face, "Janet Stone. You breathe one word to those kids about me and Cliff. Or anybody or anything. You breathe one word anywhere, anytime, anybody." She pauses, panting. Her eyes glint like the red Ring in my pocket.

"And what'll you do, Marigold Stass?"

"Why, I'll tell them all about you!"

Holy trout! Does she know? Has she guessed? I step in real close. Anyone seeing us would think we were best friends telling secrets. I whisper, "What'll you tell them about me?"

"Why, just everything. I know all about you, Janet Stone."

"What do you know about me?"

"Everything. I'll tell everybody. Nobody will ever speak to you again."

Nose to nose, we glare at each other. I'm panting now, too, and I prickle and blush, but not from shyness. From rage.

Marigold doesn't know. She can't know. I thrust a hand into my pocket and grip the Ring down there at the bottom. Its hard edges strengthen me.

I whisper, "Nobody speaks to me now. You go right ahead, tell everybody everything. And I'll tell Cute Irene and Tough Jessie and Fat Tunie all about you unless—"

"Unless what?"

"Unless you quit boasting! Marigold Stass, your boasting makes me sick! Next time you boast a word I'll tell Tough Jessie—"

Marigold swings her shoulder bag hard against my arm. It hurts. She glares. I glare, and rub my arm. We back off.

I swing around and march off the wrong way, back toward home.

I swing around again.

Marigold points her nose to the sky and heads for school.

I follow, as I have followed her so many times along this road. But this time it's OK.

It looks as if Marigold and I will never be friends, but for once she knows I'm *somebody*. My name is Janet Stone, and I'm here in Winterfield with her.

Holy trout, does she know it!

Till I can ditch this ring I'll settle for that.

*M*onday evening when Jackie and I walk in his yard Mr. Flower is brushing Pearl. Pearl looks at us softly through his silky forelock and mutters. I hug his neck and he lays his head on my shoulder.

Jackie hands Mr. Flower the bunch of daffodils she picked by our front porch.

"Mr. Flower," she says, "we've come to talk about Jannie's job."

Mr. Flower looks into the daffodils. He murmurs, "A host of golden daffodils," from his school poem.

"Yes. Your grandmother Cook planted these."

"A poet could not but be gay," Mr. Flower quotes again, "in such a jocund company!" He does not look gay. He looks bowed right down with sorrow.

Jackie tries again. "Mr. Flower, it's about Jannie's job."

"Huh. Job? Well. You know I can't keep my Pearl.

No excuse to keep him. He was for Arthur."

Jackie knows about the angry and final departure of Arthur and Family. She doesn't believe it's final. She insists they'll be back when they've cooled off. But she didn't see them leave. I did.

Mr. Flower looks across the flowers at Jackie and tries to smile. He asks, "What am I going to do now with this beautiful little pony?"

She says, "Mr. Flower, you love Pearl."

"That's darned true."

"Jannie knows someone besides Arthur you can share him with."

Mr. Flower turns sad eyes to me. "Who?"

"Mr. Flower," I say, "it's Frankie Stass."

"Frankie Stass," he repeats, as though he can't think who that may be. Today Mr. Flower seems slower and thinner than he did on Sunday.

"Next door," Jackie reminds him.

I say, "Pearl likes Frankie. And Frankie loves Pearl!"

Jackie says, "We figure Frankie can ride Pearl for you, and Jannie can still help with the other chores. And you can keep Pearl."

"I'd sure like that." Mr. Flower gazes into his daffodils. "But how do I . . . talk to this Frankie Stass?"

Jackie gives him a sharp look I'm glad he doesn't see. She says, "You can go right next door right this minute."

"Stass. Haven't seen Stass in years and years. Not since my Rosy ate his mother's tulips."

"Mr. Flower," I ask, "are you shy?"

He smiles at me through the daffodils. "You mightn't think it," he says, "but I'm shy as a deer!"

"That's OK," I tell him. "I'm shy, too."

Jackie snorts and tosses her braid back. "OK," she says, taking charge. "We'll go next door with you, Mr. Flower. Right now," she says, looking at me. "We'll all three go next door right now, this minute."

30

*H*oly trout, am I glad I kept quiet about Cliff all day, like Mr. Flower said!

It was hard. At one point Cute Irene asked Marigold how was Cliff, and it almost burst out of me there and then. But Marigold just shrugged, so I bit my tongue. Later Irene said to Jessie, "Guess Cliff and Marigold broke up, huh?" I walked by and heard and kept walking. It was one of the hardest things I've ever done! And am I glad now!

Nobody in Winterfield uses their front door. Mr. Flower and Jackie and I turned up at the Stasses' kitchen door, me hiding behind Jackie, and they let us in. Mr. Stass never said boo about any goat eating tulips. He just turned to Frankie and asked if he wanted the Pearl job, and of course Frankie did. He ran right off to see Pearl.

I looked around for someplace to hide, and there was Marigold behind me.

She said "Come up to my room" in a friendly sort of voice. I swallowed a big lump of surprise and went.

And now I'm swallowing more lumps of surprise, looking at the snapshots pinned all over Marigold's walls.

There's the Cliff birthday snaps she showed at school. There's Frankie on Pearl. There's Thunder eating a sandwich with Sophie in the snow, Cliff boring a maple, Tunie bubbling gum, Irene smirking, Jessie barking laughter. There I am, on a very scruffy Pearl, in snow.

I ask her, "Marigold, did you take all these pictures?"

" 'Course." She sprawls on the unmade bed and pats the mattress for me to sit down. Cautiously, I ease down beside her.

I say, "I do pictures too. Only I draw mine."

"Yeah? You ever draw me?"

"Um, yes." (Several times.)

"Ever draw Irene and the other kids?"

"Sort of." (I drew them once as Dog, Cat, and Rabbit.)

"Hey, I'd like to see those!"

"Well . . ."

"If you asked me over to see your stuff, maybe the kids wouldn't call you 'Stuck-up Janet' anymore."

"Holy trout! Me, stuck-up?" I thought I was Lone-

"It worked pretty good for a while. But it was wearing thin, you know?"

I nod. "Everybody's tired of it."

"Right. Me, too. And now I don't know how to be friends with Tunie, after she stole my Ring."

"But Tunie didn't steal your Ring." It's out of my mouth, I can't take it back.

Marigold studies my face. I blush and prickle as though I'm talking to a brand-new stranger.

I want to say, "I did it myself," but the words won't come. So I reach in my jeans pocket and pull out the Ring, and drop it on the mattress between us.

Marigold's eyes make saucers. We stare down at the silly, sparkling plastic toy, Cliff's Friendship Ring.

In the silence we hear Mr. Flower say under the window, "Cabbage worms. My Connie made a cabbage worm spray that worked. I'll show you how."

And Jackie asks, "Where's Jannie gone?"

Marigold murmurs, "You. You, all along." Marigold chuckles.

Cautiously, I chuckle.

Marigold laughs.

Laughter whoops out of my stomach.

We laugh till we roll off the bed and curl on the r, clutching our stomachs. When I can almost talk isper, "Maria?" Now, how did that slip out? Mar-'s nothing like Maria. Or is she?

some Janet, Janet Left Out, maybe Dumb Janet. But Stuck-up Janet, never!

"Well, sure," Marigold explains, matter-of-factly. "You look at everybody like they aren't there."

"I do?"

"Yeah. And you never speak to anybody. Never smile. That's why they call you 'Stuck-up.' "

"Holy trout, I'm new around here! You ever been new in school, Marigold?"

"No. I've lived in Winterfield all my life, and so have all my folks, forever."

"OK, that's it. You don't know what it's like—"

"But Tunie does. Tunie sort of likes you, even you are stuck-up."

"I'm not! I'm just . . . well, I'm shy." There. T' out.

"And Irene was new last year. That's . . .' gold's voice trails off. She looks out the windo at the floor. "That's why I made up the Cli

"What?"

"See, I've lived here forever. But Tur and some others came here from cities. ford. New York."

"So?"

Marigold sighs. "So I wanted th riously."

"They did that, all right!"

floc

I wł

igolo

"Huh?"

"I mean Marigold."

"Ha ha! What? Ha ha ha!"

"You want to walk to school tomorrow with me?"

"Well, I don't know." We sit up against the bed, panting. "See, that's my alone time. My only alone time all day."

"Oh." I never thought of that. I've always had plenty of alone time.

"But just for tomorrow . . . that would give the kids a jolt, wouldn't it! Oh wow!" Marigold starts to laugh again, and clutches her stomach.

Down outside, Jackie calls, "Jannie! We better start home."

"Here," says Marigold. "You keep it." She hands me the gleaming red-blue Ring. "Peace Ring."

"Oh. OK. Sure." I push it onto my little finger, the only finger it fits. We rest against the bed, watching it gleam.

Down below, Jackie calls, "Jannie!"

"OK," I croak. "I'm coming. Coming!" I tell Marigold, "See you tomorrow."

* * * * * * * * * * * * * *31*

*W*e three hurry home down Old King's
Road. Jackie swings along fast, braid bouncing down
her back. She wants to get home by dark.

I lag behind with Mr. Flower. He hobbles along as
fast as he can. My stomach still aches from laughing.
But I feel light, walking along with no stolen Ring in
my pocket! I feel . . . thin! I hold up my hand to watch
my Peace Ring glimmer in the last sunlight.

Jackie halts. "Listen!" she orders us.

We listen.

Something in the darkening woods goes bump,
crash, bump.

I whisper, "Maybe it's a bear!"

Bump, it sounds nearer. Crack, it leaps into the
middle of Old King's Road.

It stops stiff and fixes us with bright, dark eyes. It
raises one forefoot and a shining white tail. It's a deer.

It leaps across the road into woods. We watch its

white tail bounce twice among trees, and it's gone.

A man from Mars might look at you like that, then whirl his spaceship back to Mars.

"Aha!" says Jackie. "Another one's coming."

Pound, pound, come hoofbeats along the road. I say, "That's Pearl."

They canter toward us around the bend, Thunder and Frankie and Pearl. Did I think I had to help Frankie mount, and bridle Pearl for him? I should have remembered that Frankie is a Stass.

He rides proudly. Pearl's snowy mane floats on air like dandelion fluff. Thunder bounds beside them like their shadow.

Rejoicing, they canter past us and around the next bend.

Mr. Flower clears his throat. "Jannie," he says, "did I ever tell you how my Stephen loved pets?"

I start to say yes, but he goes right on—

"One time he brought a newborn fawn in the kitchen at your house. Said, 'This is our new pet.' "

I start to say, "I know, you told me," but he goes right on telling the story. And I listen like a granddaughter, because I know grandfathers do repeat stories.